# Teapots, Buttons, Memi and Me

## Lisa Rose Bauer

ISBN: **1495202763**

ISBN 13: **9781495202766**

Library of Congress Control Number: **2014900943**

CreateSpace Independent Publishing Platform

North Charleston, South Carolina

*Grandmother is a little bit parent, a little bit teacher,*
*and a little bit best friend…*
*author unknown*


In memory of Rose, my grandmother. She always
knew and was always there—
even now.

# Chapter One

"Poppy?" Sophia paused. "Will everything be the same as last summer? Things look the same."

"Not sure, missy, I'm just not sure," said Poppy as he tousled his granddaughter's curly hair.

Sophia and her grandfather walked in silence on the shell path leading toward the beach cottages. Every summer one grandchild was invited to stay at Poppy and Memi's cottage before the rest of the family, the cousins, aunts, and uncles, all arrived a few days later. This year it was Sophia's turn. But she wished more than anything that it wasn't. She heard her parents' car tires crunch over the cracked oyster shells on the long driveway behind her. Until Monday. That's a long time. She turned over her shoulder and saw Mom's arm waving out of the car window. She almost let go of Poppy's hand and ran back toward them. But she kept holding on.

"Your friend Thomas and his family will be here late tonight I hear. I am sure you'll spend time exploring like you two always do," said Poppy.

"I guess so." *At least something will be the same*, Sophia thought. Thomas and his family had been vacationing at the same beach cottages for as long as Sophia and her family. Thomas and Sophia were summer friends. She looked forward to seeing him every year.

Just past a cluster of slender white birch trees, Poppy and Memi's cottage came into sight. It still looked the same, bleached and weathered white with a bold and bright periwinkle front door. A basket of colorful petunias spilled over in greeting as if to say *welcome, welcome*.

"Poppy, can't we walk to the beach first? I don't want to go in yet. Not without Memi. I think I'll stay on the porch instead. Yep, that's what I will do, stay here on the porch," Sophia said as she plopped right there on the step.

"It's OK. Yes, let's just sit here for a while. And anyway, I want to give you something," Poppy said as he walked into the cottage, the screen door slamming after him. Sophia sat restlessly on the lopsided front step. She looked around to confirm that everything really did look the same. Tessie's garden in the next yard over the little fence was brimming again with fat, red tomatoes, heavy to be picked. Just like last summer. Mr. Reuben's little fishing boat rested in its same spot in the yard across the street. Poppy came back outside and placed a brown package next to Sophia on the uneven step.

"Here you go, this is for you," Poppy explained while backing down the steps to stand on the stone pathway to the cottage.

"What is it, Poppy? It's not my birthday or Christmas." Sophia looked puzzled.

"You will see. You will see. Open it whenever you'd like."

Sophia picked up the box and shook it just a bit. She did not hear anything except for a slight little jangle. Sophia sat next to the wrapped package for a long time. The afternoon sun started to descend toward early evening. Memi used to call late afternoon *that time of day*. She described the sunlight as *gorgeous, lush,* and *surreal*. Memi would close her eyes and take in a big giant inhale of salt air and wind and laughter from the beach.

When the sun fell behind the little cove across the street, Sophia lifted the box and placed it on her lap. She tore the thick brown paper away from the box and then lifted the lid. She reached in her hand and plowed through the packing hay with her fingers. She felt a smooth, cool surface and again heard a light rattle and clank.

Sophia scooped down to the bottom with one hand. With the other hand she guided the gift up through the straw-like nest. As she pulled it up, there it was like a treasure from a happier time. A china teapot. One of Memi's lovely teapots. Sophia lightly touched the soft blue pansies delicately painted on the plump "belly" of the teapot. Then she dug into the bottom of the box again, hoping there'd be something else there. Knowing there'd be something else. At the bottom of the box she felt tissue paper with a softness tucked inside it. Before she even fished it out, Sophia knew, she knew. With a quick yank she pulled up the package. The tissue unfolded and out spilled the cornflower-blue calico apron. Sophia grabbed up the apron and held it just beneath her nose and breathed in deep and full. She heard Memi's voice in her head saying, *Here you go, child, you wear*

*the apron. Let's make some bread. And while it's baking
we can pull down the jar of buttons…*

Sophia remembered that while the bread was baking
Memi would pull down an antique preserve jar filled
with buttons of all shapes and colors and sizes. Memi
would shake the jar like a maraca on her way back to
the table with all the buttons swishing a *cha-cha-cha*.
Among them a red caboose, a white daisy, a green tur-
tle, an antique copper button. Memi spilled the buttons
across the table top and the two made up stories about the
clothing the buttons once were sewed to and about the
people who wore them. What were their names? Where
did they live? What did their dresses and coats look
like? When the baking timer went off, Memi and Sophia
would scoop up the dozens and dozens of buttons and
move the jar to the center of the table as a centerpiece.
Sophia would watch Memi pull the loaf of bread from
the oven and place it on the countertop. Never a small
slice; Memi always carved a big first chunk and brought
the china plates to the table. The butter and strawberry
jam oozed together. Memi poured hot tea from one of
her china teapots and the two sipped tea and talked and
laughed.

The memory made Sophia smile, but also feel a little sad. She gently shook the teapot and heard a light chinking from inside. She pinched the knob of the lid and slowly lifted it and peeked in. There nested in the belly of the teapot were Memi's little things. An antique brass key. A piece of sapphire sea glass. A mother-of-pearl button. A little glass ladybug. Sophia reached in and carefully scooped up the little things. She held them at eye level on her outstretched palm and remembered.

Each morning Memi pulled the teapot from the little shelf above her kitchen sink. She placed it on the counter. She took down her blue flowered apron from the peg by the window. Sometimes it looked like Memi was dreaming as she tied her apron strings in the back while looking out the window to the ocean, maybe to another time. And one by one Memi placed each of the four little things into the front apron pocket. Always the same. Every day.

# Chapter Two

Sophia saw Poppy across the street at the little fishing dock behind Mr. Reuben's house. She didn't notice that he had left her sitting on the porch. He was tending his fishing pole and looking out at the ocean. Was he missing Memi too? Was he lonely? Sophia gathered the wrapping hay, the apron, and the teapot back up. When she picked up the box it tilted way over and out spilled one more thing. It was a small brown package the size of a school book. There, written on the outside of the package in beautifully scripted letters, was her name, SOPHIA. Sophia slid her fingers under the tape at the corners and opened the paper. Inside was a beautiful notebook, with a thick cardboard cover, decorated in a multicolored swirl of paisley pinks, blues, and greens. Sophia opened the book and saw Memi's calligraphy-style writing in a message on the inside cover. Her heart beat so fast she felt it thump in her chest and her throat.

My dearest Sophia,

Remember the day last summer when we visited the village at Indigo Beach? We stopped into the little paper shop and looked at cards and notepaper and pretty wrappings. And I bought this lovely journal. I hoped to write everything down, all the stories of the little things. But now I give the book to you, my memory book, and hope that you will write down the stories for me as they come into your mind and heart. Please keep the apron and the teapot and, of course, the little things, too. Remember them always for me. The key and the sea glass. The ladybug and the button. In life, the little things always matter most of all, the blessings we have and give to each other. May your life bring you peace and balance and hope...and someday may you find your own way. I will be with you always.

Memi

Sophia slowly fanned the pages of the book. Every page was blank. Not a word. She gathered up the teapot and the apron. Sophia looked for Poppy and at first could not find him. She then saw him standing right next door, picking tomatoes from Tessie's garden. He spotted Sophia and said, "Look at these. We can put them in our salad tonight. Sound good?"

Sophia hesitated, then nodded and said, "OK, Poppy." She felt confused. She never remembered him picking tomatoes from Tessie's garden before. Tessie usually brought her vegetables over in a brown paper bag and gave them to Memi.

Sophia paused on the front step. A worried feeling came over her, but she did not know exactly why. Just then, as if the August wind turned her around, she walked into the little cottage to find her room in the back left corner. Sophia placed the teapot and the apron next to her bed on the old nightstand. She arranged them perfectly and sat on the bed looking out the window with the book on her lap. She took a pen from the nightstand drawer. On the first page she wrote in big letters MEMI'S MEMORY BOOK. Sophia closed the book when she heard Poppy call for supper. She whispered into the quiet of the cottage room, "How can it be the same without you, Mem?"

## Chapter Three

Their forks clicked and clanked. Poppy and Sophia sipped their water at the same time making noise, but otherwise they sat in silence. Sophia wondered if Poppy would start talking. But he did not. He just scooped salad with those big juicy tomato slices into her salad bowl. Memi would have been talking by now, that's for sure, Sophia thought. They would have planned the whole three days from morning to night. Memi would have told her about all the families she saw all summer at the beach. And Memi would have known that Sophia really did not like tomatoes.

"Poppy, I am tired. Can I just go to my room?" asked Sophia as she dried the last dish and placed it in Memi's cupboard.

"That's fine, I am tired too." Poppy patted Sophia's head and went into the little front room where an old television showed the evening news. He placed his reading glasses on and picked up a book from the table by his chair.

Sophia went back to her little room. She knew it wasn't her room. Her cousins and brother shared it, too. But for these three days it was her room. All by herself. Sophia heard thunder in the distance. Late August was so humid that storms often passed through the beach. She looked out her window and could see heat lightning illuminating the rolling ocean. She touched the memory book and moved her fingers over the paisley swirls. She picked up the book and opened to the first blank page. *Oh Mem, I am not a writer. I am not sure I can do this.* But she knew she had to try because Memi asked her to and believed she could.

She took the lid off the teapot and reached in. She pulled up the old brass key.

*Tell me the story of the key again, Mem, please.*
Sophia would come in closer on the porch swing and
Memi would pull the key from her apron pocket.

When my father was a little boy his father owned a fruit
and vegetable store on Pine Street. Everyone would come to
the store on Saturdays especially, because on that day Angelo
had his produce set out on carts in front of the market. Let-
tuce, eggplants, carrots, peaches, plums, basil. He sold olive
oil and big loaves of bread and cheese. This key used to open
the front door of the store, Sophia. My father, Joseph, used
to hide under the fruit stands and just listen and watch all of
the people hustle and bustle. The market was my family's start
in America. One day there was an explosion in the market and
then a fire. Everything burned. Angelo lost everything. His
market was gone. The only thing left was this key.

Sophia always felt sad when she heard the story. But
Memi would say, *Sophia, don't be sad. Angelo and his
family got to start over. He took his family and moved up
north to find other work.* Memi held the key everyday
to remind her of new starts even when things seemed
hopeless.

Sophia placed the pen on the table and looked at her words. She dated the bottom of the passage, August 12, and closed the book. Sophia looked at her bed covered in the white eyelet quilt that Memi had made herself. Memi always tucked Sophia into her cottage bed; a clean cottony smell surrounded her before she fell asleep with her grandmother right there. But Sophia could not fall asleep on that first night. She got up and sat by the window to watch the lightning some more. She held the apron over her lap. She heard talking and even laughing. Sophia went to the other window of her room and saw the little fire pit glowing on Tessie's patio. Tessie was sitting in one of the chairs facing Sophia's window. The light was very dim. Who was the other person? She almost thought it sounded like Poppy, but it couldn't be. He was in the front room watching the news. Sophia tiptoed out to the center of the cottage and turned the corner to the front room.

"Poppy?" she called. He did not answer. The TV was off and the book was closed. Sophia's heart started beating and her head felt funny. She quickly walked, almost slid, back to her bedroom window. She said the words, but no sound came out. *Poppy? Is that you?* She stared at the two people sitting next to each other in front of the dimming fire. The other person placed a piece of firewood into the pit. The man laughed and just then the new piece of wood caught ablaze and shone on the two people. Tessie and Poppy. Laughing and talking. *I must be dreaming*, thought Sophia, her mind racing like beach wind before a storm. Is this a dream? *Ask questions, ask questions. I am twelve years old. Yes. I am Sophia. Yes. I have long brown curly hair. Too much of it. Yes. I am staying with Poppy until everyone gets here on Monday. Yes.* All yeses! This was *not* a dream. Poppy *was* sitting at night sharing the little fire with Tessie. Memi's friend Tessie. My Auntie Tessie. *For sure nothing is the same.* Sophia tucked the apron under her chin. She could hardly catch her breath, but finally, finally fell asleep.

## Chapter Four

Sophia woke up to banging on the porch door. She never slept that late at the beach. Ten in the morning. There was no air moving anywhere. Just hot, sticky, heavy air all around. She heard talking in the kitchen and pulled the pillow over her head. *I cannot possibly go out and eat breakfast with Poppy. Not today, not any day,* she thought. Sophia tucked herself behind the door of her room, but stuck her head out a bit to hear the talking in the kitchen.

"Mr. Thomas, good morning. When did you get here?" Poppy said cheerfully. Sophia thought it was more cheerfulness than she usually received in the morning. Poppy was always so quiet when they were together.

"Hi, Mr. Poppy, we got here late sometime last night. I'm not sure what time. I fell asleep in the car as soon as we left home. But I'm not sure how, since Avery was crying almost the whole way," said Thomas. Thomas always called Poppy, Mr. Poppy. And Poppy always called Thomas, Mr. Thomas. It was their little joke. Thomas and his family had started visiting his grandparents at their beach cottage when he was five years old. His cottage was down the beach path from Poppy's. Memi and Thomas's grandmother, Elizabeth, worked together years ago at the dress factory that Memi's uncle owned. They had stayed friends ever since. Even though the two friends moved to different states, this was the one week out of the year that Memi and Elizabeth's families spent with their children and grandchildren at the beach.

"Is Sophia here yet, Mr. Poppy?" asked Thomas.

"Sure is. She'll be happy to see you. Haven't seen her yet this morning, though. Not since supper time last night. I'll let her know you're here," Poppy explained.

Just then Sophia burst out of the room wearing shorts and a tank top over her bathing suit. She had a beach bag in her hand and flip-flops on, with her long spirally curls every which way beneath the turquoise baseball hat on her head.

"Hi, Thomas," Sophia said before she even turned the corner to the kitchen.

"Hi, Sophia!" said Thomas.

"We'll be at the beach all day, right, Thomas?" Sophia declared as she grabbed a banana and bottled water from the counter.

"Uhhh, yep. We will, Mr. Poppy."

Sophia then ushered Thomas out the door and off the front porch as if they were late to get somewhere.

"Wow, Soph, what a rush you're in. Where you going so fast?" asked Thomas as they finally slowed down near Thomas's cottage. He could hear Avery crying again.

"Oh, not again. My mom thinks she has an ear infection. Wish Avery could talk to tell her. This screaming is making me crazy," said Thomas. "I wish I had three days alone here with my grandpa and grandma."

"Oh, no you don't. I can't wait for the others to get here," Sophia almost growled the words.

"I thought you loved your first days alone here? What happened?" asked Thomas.

"Where do I start?" Sophia asked.

The two friends walked past Thomas's cottage until the crying faded. They walked in silence up the path to the main beach and were welcomed by a swoosh of hot summer air and the sound of crashing waves beginning to descend to low tide. Early beachgoers were already staking out their spaces on the beach on the hot August day. Thomas's dad already had their spot and was constructing the little tent they used to protect baby Avery from the sun. Thomas walked toward his father and pointed to Sophia. He waved and Sophia waved back. Thomas pointed to the jetty. Sophia guessed he was telling his father they'd be searching for sea glass. On their first day together, Sophia and Thomas always went to the shallow cove of ocean water near the drawbridge. That's where the best sea glass was always found. Thomas loved drawing and painting. He painted beautiful scenes of the ocean and sea glass and all kinds of boats that he sent to Sophia in the winter months when they did not see each other.

Sophia and Thomas walked to the end of the shoreline and then went left when they reached the jetty. They walked through the tall beach grasses, so dry the stalks prickled their bare legs. Just over the bluff was Indigo Cove, filled with an almost magical, crystal-colored water that was always calm and swirled in delicate patterns. During high tide, when the ocean waves crested and rolled forward, the cove disappeared. Only in low tide conditions was Indigo Cove even reachable. The cove was so peaceful and still that people always returned to seek its sea glass, which was known to have strong, calming powers.

"Looks like just the two of us to start the day," said Thomas.

"Good, we'll get the best pieces, then," said Sophia as they pulled out their little tin buckets, which they used to hold the day's treasures.

"How come you left the cottage so fast today, Soph?" asked Thomas.

"Oh nothing, no reason really," answered Sophia, not knowing how to explain how mad she was at Poppy.

"You seemed like you didn't want to talk to Mr. Poppy," said Thomas as he crouched down and sifted through a raggle-taggle of shells and seaweed and beach wood.

"Everything is different without Memi here. I thought I would be OK here with just Poppy until everyone else gets here. But he is sooooo quiet," explained Sophia as she kicked her toes up and splashed the crystal water.

"Yeah, my granddad is quiet, too," said Thomas, bent at the waist and looking straight down toward his feet as he explored the shallow water and shore.

"I just miss Memi and how much she used to talk to me. And last night I saw…" Just as Sophia was going to share that she saw Poppy visiting Tessie's patio, a group of kids from the cottages closer to the bayside waved and screamed from the top of the bluff. Thomas and Sophia waved them down to the cove.

"But it's OK, Thomas. Soon everyone else will be here. Hey, look at this piece," and Sophia held up a smooth, white-frosted piece of sea glass. She knew it wasn't a rare find, but mentioning it stopped any further discussion of Poppy.

After a long morning of sea glass hunting, Thomas and Sophia headed to Thomas's family beach camp. Sophia looked around near the main beach flagpole where her family usually spent their days at the beach. Some other family was in that spot today and probably would be tomorrow. But soon all of her cousins and both families would be together. Dad and Uncle Teddy would get up early enough to create the day's family beach camp.

They would lay blankets down and poke umbrellas into the sand. Next, they'd place beach chairs in a big, wide circle. But for two more days it was still just Poppy and Sophia.

Sophia placed a hand over her eyes. The glare from the setting sun made it hard to see. She looked up to the benches at the end of the wooden pathway. That's where Poppy usually liked to sit and watch everyone. Last year he had stopped walking through the sand and to the beach circle where everyone gathered. As Sophia watched, a family, with what seemed like a hundred pounds of beach gear, crossed in front of the bench area. Kids, wagons, parents, coolers, umbrellas, towels, boogie boards. Everyone had something en route to stake a spot on the still-crowded late-day beach. When the family had cleared out of the way, Sophia saw Poppy up there standing in front of a bench. He seemed to be looking for her. Poppy knew the spot where Thomas's family always set up for the day. Sophia's heart cracked a little. She could not help but head over to tell Poppy she was OK and with Thomas.

"Be right back," she said to Thomas or anyone listening at his family's busy beach spot. Sophia knew more than anything that she did not want to see Poppy, let alone talk to him. But the way he was looking back and forth made her think he might be worried. She walked with her head down to block the wind and the glare. *What will we talk about? Did he see me in the window last night? Does he know I saw him at Tessie's?* As Sophia made it up the little incline to the benches, Poppy spoke.

"Hello, missy, haven't seen much of you today? Everything OK?" Poppy's tall frame blocked the sun and everything around him.

"Thomas and I were looking for sea glass. And then I had lunch on his blanket with his family." Sophia did not look up at him. "Is it time to go?"

"You can stay a while longer. Then we'll go home and have supper. I invited Tessie to join us since her family won't be here for a couple of days. And you have not seen her yet. Or have you?"

"No, I haven't seen Tessie yet," Sophia said, looking down at her toes as she buried them in and out of the sand. Sophia wanted to say, *Oh, I saw Tessie. And I saw you. Both of you whispering and talking by the fire pit last night*. But she did not say anything like that.

"Can I go back to Thomas's now?" Sophia was at Poppy's side now, looking out at the ocean.

"Yes, I'll wait here for you. Another thirty minutes OK?" Poppy asked.

"Yep, that's fine, Poppy," said Sophia. But what Sophia thought was something else altogether. *No, Poppy, it is absolutely not fine that Tessie is coming to supper. When Memi was here last summer that was fine. But without Memi here. Not fine!* Her head was screaming the words on the inside. When she looked back over her shoulder to see if Poppy had sat down, she could not believe what she saw. Tessie had just arrived at the benches and had sat down next to Poppy. Again, sitting and talking. *About what? What could they possibly be talking about?*

Sophia raced back to the blanket and dug into her beach bag. She knew she only had a few minutes, but she had a remembering and had to write it down for Memi. *Poppy might forget you, Memi, but I will not,* she thought as she pulled out the memory book.

Memi,

I remember walking with you to Indigo Cove. We would look for sea glass. I always loved the story you told of the sapphire sea glass you found near your Grandma Anna's beach. All your cousins would walk to the beach before supper and explore and sing and be silly. You loved that beach so much. The sapphire glass in the teapot reminded you of Anna's house and big family dinners sitting under Grandpa Jimmy's grapevines on very hot summer nights. You loved your family and sharing times together.

After she was finished writing, Sophia looked up and saw Thomas staring at her.

"What are you looking at, Thomas? What's wrong?" Sophia asked in a tone that surprised even her.

"Nothing's wrong with me. But are you OK?" asked Thomas, his fair skin red from the day's sun and his blond hair all tousled in the beach wind.

"No, I'm not OK. I am mad at my Poppy. But I have to go now. He is making supper and he invited a *guest*." Sophia emphasized the word guest as she almost hissed it. She would not identify to Thomas the name of the guest. She felt funny since Thomas's grandparents knew her Poppy and Tessie, too. All the grandparents knew each other from when they first bought their cottages years ago.

"He's waving me over, I have to go now," Sophia said as she put the memory book and her towel and hat in her bag. She put on her tank top and shorts. Then she said goodbye to Thomas and thank you to his family and walked back up to the benches.

## Chapter Five

Sophia made her way, weaving through the patches of beach blankets up toward the benches.

"I'm here," Sophia announced as she stood like a cement statue in front of Poppy and Tessie.

"Yes, I see that," said Poppy. "And to my left is Tessie, remember her?" Poppy said, smiling and gesturing toward Tessie. Sophia had not seen Poppy smile so big since she arrived. Or heard him make any jokes.

"Well, come on over here and give your Auntie Tessie a big hug for goodness sake," Tessie said as she received Sophia up in the scoop of Poppy's motion to nudge her over.

"Hi, Auntie Tessie," Sophia said flatly. She had no other words. Although Tessie was not really Sophia's aunt, she and her husband Max were such close friends with Memi and Poppy that the children and grandchildren all called them Auntie and Uncle.

"That's it from my little girl? Thought I'd see you this morning. I had chocolate chip muffins just baked for you." Tessie rubbed sand off of Sophia's shoulders and arms. But Sophia still stood statue-like with her thin arms straight down at her legs. She always stopped by Tessie's on the first morning for a treat, but there was no way she could have done that today.

"I had to meet Thomas to go hunting for sea glass. Sorry." Sophia could not say that she was mad at Tessie and Poppy for what she had seen last night.

"Let's head back so we can start supper," said Poppy. He let Tessie and Sophia walk ahead.

Sophia then waited and Poppy joined them. Then she fell back in her step and let Poppy and Tessie go ahead. *Let them walk since they have so much to talk about,* Sophia yelled inside. Sophia slapped her flip-flops on the path back toward the circle of cottages. Tessie looked back and then up at Poppy. With the beach wind against her face Sophia could not hear every word, but she thought she heard Tessie say, *John, she seems mad about something.*

When they got back to the cottages, Sophia promptly went to the outdoor shower stall. Memi called it the *al fresco* shower. Everyone loved to look up at the clouds while washing and shampooing. Once inside the wooden stall and away from the world, Sophia inhaled, sucking all the air that she could fit into her lungs. She realized that she probably did not breathe the entire walk back from the beach. Along with her huge exhale came drippy, sniffly tears. *Why did you have to leave, Memi? Why?* She squeezed her eyes shut tight and faced directly into the shower stream. When she opened her eyes she looked into the little mirror Memi had placed in the wooden shower area. Sophia saw her red, puffy eyes and went closer to look. When she did, that's when she saw it. There in the corner near the shampoo bottle and the soap dish was a little ladybug, swirling in a few drops of shower water. Sophia laughed and cried at the same time, saying, *Thanks, Memi,* into the wide open air and into the wind.

After Sophia dried off and wrapped the beach towel around her, she tiptoed into the cottage and went straight to her room. She heard Tessie and Poppy talking on the porch but ignored them. She put on a soft jersey sundress and sat on the edge of the bed. Opening the memory book, Sophia wrote:

Dear Memi,

I remember sitting with you last summer. You had just started feeling tired and not so well. Now I know why you told me the story of your friend Eva. You always said she left way too early. You said Eva was the very best friend anyone could ever ask for. She had a big, giant heart and made everyone feel so special. She loved to laugh and cook and be with the people she loved. You became friends from the very first day you worked together in the factory sewing dresses a long time ago. The winter Eva got sick, you visited her and you both sat by the fireplace. You drank tea and ate shortbread and talked for a long time. She would rest and you tucked the blanket under her feet and around her shoulders. She whispered to you, "I promise I won't be too far away. Here, take this and remember me. Think of me whenever you are sad or lonely. Think of the laughter and our friendship."

And then Eva handed you the little glass ladybug. I saw a ladybug today in the al fresco shower. Maybe you are not too far away. I miss you, Mem. Poppy is so quiet. And there are some things happening at the beach cottage you would be mad about. It's Poppy and Tessie. I think they like each other. But I can't tell you why. And now I have to go eat supper with them. But I wish it was you at the table instead.

 Chapter Six

"John, would you like another slice?" Tessie held up the peach pie a little as if to say, look how delicious, as she lightly touched the top of Poppy's hand.

"No thanks, Tess. I'm full from supper, but, hmm-mm that first piece was delicious, wasn't it, Sophia?" nudged Poppy as he tapped his granddaughter on the elbow.

Sophia could hardly breathe, let alone speak. She could not believe her eyes or ears. John. Tess. *He is Poppy and you are Tessie,* Sophia wanted to shout. *And why are you offering my Poppy another slice of peach pie in his own kitchen? Memi used to do that. Not you!* Somehow Sophia finally found her words.

"Yes, the pie was good. Can I be excused now?" Sophia looked down at her half-eaten slice of pie. She really did love Auntie Tessie's pies- and she always asked for seconds. But that was last summer, when Memi was still there sitting at the table, when they *all* laughed together. Not secretly out on Tessie's patio at night.

"Sophia, why don't you sit for a while? Are you feeling too old now to sit and talk with us old folks?" Poppy inquired.

"Oh, John, just let her go now. She has things to do I am sure in her own room, right Sophia?" said Tessie as she stood up to begin clearing the mismatched dishes from the table.

"Well, OK then, Sophia, you can go along. I didn't forget that tomorrow is your last own day. I thought we could do something together. Maybe go on a whale watch? I think I can still handle that, don't you think so, Tess?"

*Oh, here he goes again. John and Tess. Why is he asking Tessie if he can still go on a whale watch?* Sophia loved whale watching, loved the chance to witness the beauty of those majestic whales out in their own ocean. Sophia thought watching them was one of the most peaceful things in the world. "I don't think so, Poppy.

I think Thomas and I are going back to the cove. It's low tide in the morning," explained Sophia. She knew she could tell Thomas she was going on a whale watch instead. But Sophia just could not say yes. *I don't want to be with John and Tess on a whale watch*, she thought.

"Well, maybe we can all go when the others get here, then," said Poppy as he stood and pushed his chair back on the old gold-toned linoleum floor. "I am going to help Mr. Reuben across the way with his boat. He asked me earlier. Sophia, Tessie will stay here for a while, OK?"

"That's OK, Poppy, I really don't need a *babysitter*." As she emphasized the word, she quickly looked at Tessie and then at the floor. "You're only across the road." Sophia wondered if hearing that word *babysitter* felt as bad as saying it. Tessie was never considered a babysitter. She was a wonderful family friend. Her Auntie Tessie. But not anymore.

"I'll be across the yard if anyone needs anything," Tessie said as she took her old pie tin from the counter and walked toward the back porch door without looking at Sophia or Poppy.

"Tessie, wait, please. Sophia, you were very rude to your Aunt Tessie, now please apologize to her," said

Poppy, in the stern voice reserved only for his most angry moods.

"No, John, not now," Tessie said as she went out the door, waving the whole scene away with her hand up in the air.

"She is not my aunt, Poppy. She is no one to me. And she is absolutely not my Memi. Maybe you think so. But I don't," shouted Sophia, loud enough for anyone in the cottage circle to hear her. Including Tessie.

"Sophia, *what* is wrong with you? You have been a most rude and unfriendly little girl all day long. It's not like you at all." From the front porch, Poppy came back into the kitchen and stood at the sink basin. He looked nine feet tall with his arms folded across his chest. His hair was straggly. Sophia thought he looked very tired. But she did not give way to care. She was the one who was mad. How could he be madder?

"I saw you last night, Poppy, sitting by Tessie's cozy little fire. Laughing and talking. Tessie is not Memi. How could you sit there with Memi's friend like that? Memi would not like that. Memi is your wife, not Tessie." Sophia tried to catch her breath through her crushing tears.

"Sophia, do you think…" But before Poppy could finish Sophia raced back to her little room. She slammed the door and plunged onto the bed. She reached for the apron under her pillow. Sophia buried her face in the pillow, squeezed the apron, and screamed, "Memi, I hate them both. They forgot about you. I hate them both. I promise I will never forget about you."

# Chapter Seven

As soon as Sophia heard Poppy leave the cottage in the morning, she slipped out of her room. She stood to the side of the kitchen window, which was covered in a pale yellow gingham curtain. She wanted to be sure Poppy was clear across the road at Mr. Reuben's. The minute Sophia felt that Poppy was far enough away, she slowly walked toward Poppy's room. She stood at the doorway and looked in. The curtains were half open and with the cloudy morning, the room was dim. She tried to step over the threshold a few times, but she held back by grasping the door frame. Sophia felt like she was being pulled into the room, as if she were attached to an invisible thread.

*This is Poppy's room. I know I should not go in*, Sophia said to herself. But no sooner did she have that thought than she was inside the room. Poppy and Memi's room. Sophia's eyes went right to the dresser in the left corner of the room by the window. The faint daylight fell on the dresser area. Sophia did not see many things on the dresser, just Poppy's change dish, some lotions and medicines, his eyeglasses, and a picture frame. Sophia walked up closer to the dresser, and that's when she saw the photo. It was of Poppy and Memi in dress-up clothes, waving at the camera. They were young and smiling and looked happier than any two people she had ever seen. Sophia picked up the small frame and stared at Memi. *You were beautiful, Mem*, Sophia thought. She held the frame in the quiet of that moment. Sophia thought she heard someone walking up the path. *Please don't be Poppy.* She hastily put the photo back in its place and quickly left the room.

Sophia's heart was pounding as she launched into the kitchen. No one was there. She stood in the middle of the floor and just listened, trying to calm down. She wanted to hear Memi mixing muffins at the countertop while chattering away about something or other. Cracking eggs. Pouring milk. Mixing the flour. But instead all she heard was the silence. Sophia went to sit on the porch to wait for Thomas and to catch her breath. Poppy was still across the road with Mr. Reuben. He looked over once and waved. Sophia pretended she did not see him. She quickly looked in the direction of Tessie's cottage and saw her in the kitchen window but looked away before their eyes met. She hoped Thomas would get there soon. Sophia tapped her bare toes on the steps nervously. *Come on, Thomas, please get here before one of them tries to talk to me or asks me a question.*

Thomas appeared at the edge of the path just as Tessie opened her cottage door. Sophia didn't look over when she heard the door. Instead she bolted off the step and walked quickly to meet Thomas. She had her backpack and bucket all ready for another day at Indigo Cove. She heard Tessie's voice, but could not understand the words in all the wind. Sophia did not look back. Thomas and Sophia continued to walk toward the Cove. The day was not a sunny beach one, so there were not many families setting up.

"What happened last night at your cottage? My Gram said she heard you yelling. Were you?" Thomas looked a little worried as they walked into the cove area.

"I was so mad at Poppy and Tessie. And I still am. They have been talking a lot and spending time together," Sophia said sadly as she pulled up the hood of her sweatshirt. The August morning was unseasonably cool and the air felt soggy.

"But why are you mad?" Thomas asked.

"I just miss Memi. And I think they forgot about her," Sophia answered softly.

The two friends searched for sea glass without talking. Thomas picked up a few pieces. Sophia did not find anything new or interesting for a long time. Suddenly, something caught Sophia's eye. A little brass button swirled peacefully in a small pool of ocean water as the wind and clouds and sky all screamed storm, storm, storm. Sophia picked up the little button and placed it in her bucket.

"We better head back. The sky looks darker. My dad will be coming to look for us," said Thomas.

"But I'll have to see them if I go back. I can't go. It's supposed to be Memi in that cottage, Thomas. She always used to say, *I'll help you find your way.* And now she's gone." Sophia walked a few steps behind Thomas. She pulled the two sides of her hood together in front of her eyes to wipe the tears, to block the wind. To shut out the world.

"Sophia, come on. There's hardly anyone out here now. They'll be worried," Thomas said as he picked up the pace. The pieces of sea glass in his bucket clinked together.

"I can't go yet, Thomas. Can't we sit on the benches?" Sophia ran ahead of Thomas toward the benches.

"No, Sophia, we should head back to the cottages. I see my dad coming down the road."

The wind grew stronger and the sand started to swirl everywhere on the beach.

"Thomas, I can't go back yet, please." Sophia screamed her words against the wind.

"I am leaving *now* Sophia," Thomas yelled back.

A bolt of white lightning flashed across the ocean. The beach was empty. Sophia knew it was time to go. She was afraid of lightning and storms. But she just stood there and did not move. Thomas's father came to the end of the pathway and yelled for Sophia. Just behind him was Poppy. She saw Poppy shouting, but she could not hear anything he said. She saw his lips and mouth move, but the wind swallowed up his words. Her stomach felt sick and her heart felt like it was made of stone. She hated to see Poppy out in the wind and storm. She hated to see him worried.

Sophia bolted up the path and went past Poppy, Thomas, and his dad. She ran all the way back to the cottage circle. The rain had started to come down like ice pellets, and it hurt Sophia's skin. Just as she reached Poppy's cottage, she slipped in her wet flip-flops and fell into the side garden. Her bucket spilled over and the only thing in it fell out. The little brass button. She tried to look for the button in the muddy garden. She scooped up blobs of mud and sifted through them as if looking for a bit of gold. Through the raindrops and her tears, all a mixture, she saw Thomas's feet and looked up.

"Sophia, what are you doing?" Thomas's soaking-wet hair was plastered to the sides of his head and was down in front of his eyes.

"I lost the button I just found at the cove. I need to find it," Sophia yelled through the rainy wind.

"Mr. Poppy and my father will be coming up the path in a minute. Come on, you have to get up," Thomas pleaded with a nervous look on his face.

"Thomas. I can't. I need to find the button. Why did this have to happen? Why did any of this have to happen?"

"Sophia, come on, give me your hand," shouted Thomas. With the little energy she had left, Sophia held up her hand as her other one squished into the garden and grabbed at the earth like a bucket shovel. Once standing, Sophia quickly patted off her hands and that's when she felt it. The little brass button was pasted to her hand with mud. She smiled, plucked the button from her palm, and stuffed it into the front pocket of her drenched sweatshirt.

"Let's go," Thomas yelled into the gusting wind.

Finally, once she was up on the porch, Sophia saw Poppy walking toward the cottage. Thomas turned and ran to meet his father down the path. Sophia walked inside the cottage, went directly to her room, and closed the door. She took the button from her pocket, wiped it on her shorts, and placed it on the side table. She got out of her wet clothes and put on a dry sweatshirt and sweatpants. Sophia pulled her long wet curls into an elastic on top of her head and sat on the bed. She looked over at the memory book and knew what she would write about today. But first her heavy eyes and sheer exhaustion took over, and soon she was napping through the end of the storm.

## Chapter Eight

A sliver of light from the setting sun spilled into Sophia's room and onto her face. When she opened her eyes she had no idea what time it was. *Is this morning?* she wondered. Sophia leaned over toward the window, looked out, and realized it was the same day. There was no wind or rain. The almost-evening sky was tiered in melting ribbons of soft orange, red, and yellow.

Sophia hung her feet over the side of the bed, wondering what time it was. She walked to the door and opened it a little to listen. She did not hear Poppy or anything at all. Sophia lifted the lid of the teapot and reached in, feeling for the pearl button. When she touched it she plucked it out of the pot and held it. She picked up the memory book, her pen, and a blanket and quietly slipped out of her room.

She tiptoed through the kitchen and out onto the porch. The air was calm and fresh. Sophia could not believe that the storm had happened just that afternoon. She looked into the side garden and saw her footprints and thought again of the whole scene of rushing back from the beach. She remembered Poppy's worried look when she was still on the beach and how he shouted out for her. She squashed the thought and reminded herself that she was still mad at him. But for a second she had to remind herself why.

The sound of running water, pots and pans, and the baking timer all filled the space between Poppy's and Tessie's cottages. Sophia did not dare look up to Tessie's window. Sophia sat on Memi's blue Adirondack chair, pulled her legs up Indian style, and then covered herself with the soft blanket from her bed. She placed the memory book on her lap, opened it up, and began to write.

August 14—Dear Memi,

Today I found a button at the cove. Thomas and I go sea glass hunting, not button hunting. But today, this is what I found. It's a small brass button and is a little rusted. Not as pretty as yours, but all the way home while running through a bad storm I thought of your button in the teapot. And your story. I can still hear your story.

"When I worked in the dress factory I made pretty, silky dresses and soft, flowing blouses that were shipped by train to New York City and Chicago. I always dreamed about the ladies who wore the clothes we made. Who they were? And what were their lives like? One day my Uncle Joe asked me to take the train to New York to deliver some clothing to a new shop owner in the Garment District. I was so nervous. How would I find my way alone in such a big city? But two days later I was on a train all by myself with a satchel of dresses and blouses. I got off the train and walked out into the city and could not believe the buildings and the traffic and the people. I delivered the dresses to the shop on Seventh Avenue and Thirty-Eighth Street. The shopkeeper handed me a little cloth purse and said, 'Your Uncle Joe would like you to take a couple of dollars and buy yourself something.' There was so little money to spare, at first I could not dream of buying something for myself. But then, walking by a little vintage shop, I saw a beautiful sweater in the window. A lovely, handmade sweater of winter white with five mother-of-pearl buttons down the front and a rolled collar to hug my neck. I walked into the shop and asked to try on the sweater. I stared at myself in the big mirror of the dressing room decorated with soft lights and pretty things. I almost missed the train from Penn Station back home. Once on the train, I held the sweater wrapped in brown paper on my lap. I smiled. I always kept the last pearl button from that sweater to remember my day in New York. A day that forever reminded me that I could find my own way."

Sophia looked up from her writing and saw that it was nearly dark out. She could see Tessie sitting on her porch with a little candle flickering under a miniature hurricane shade. Sophia stood up and peeked inside the cottage. She saw Poppy dozing in the front room with the TV on, his head sagging to one side of the chair back. She thought he looked old. Just as Sophia was about to sit back down, she heard Tessie speaking in a gentle voice.

"Sophia, please…come over and sit with me for a little while?" Tessie cleared her throat after she asked the question.

Sophia stood frozen. *I can't go over there. I can't.* Yet as Sophia was thinking the words in her head, her feet were moving across the floor and off the porch. She found herself walking up the little steps to Tessie's porch. She did not speak. And neither did Tessie. Sophia sat in the chair across from Tessie.

Tessie held a small, ivory-colored note card in her hand. Without any announcement, she opened the card and began to read,

My dear friend Tessie,

How long ago that we met on that very first day sharing a sewing table. We were such young women. And to think that by chance on that first day I sat next to you, our sewing machines humming side by side. Our friendship has been a gift to me. You understood the little things, Tess. Always. I want you to hold onto this little thimble given to me by my dear Aunt Nellie so many years ago. Please, I ask you to be there for my grandchildren, especially my dear Sophia, the youngest. And I ask you as well to keep John company. As you know, he is the quiet sort. But I know he will enjoy sitting and talking with you and remembering all our good times. Someday too, please give the thimble to Sophia. I am not sure when, but you will know. Tell her I wore it when I first learned to hand stitch. How amazing that something so little can protect us and also remind us of a place long before this time. I wish you health and peace in your years ahead, As always— Olivia.

Tessie stopped reading and looked out off the porch. Sophia wiped her bubbly tears with the backs of both hands. To hear Memi's words being read into the salty breeze nearly cracked her heart, yet filled it at the same time.

"Sophia, for you," Tessie said as she handed Sophia a little midnight-blue satin pouch shaped like a miniature envelope. Tiny blue and red vines and flowers were stitched on the smooth fabric. A tiny fastener kept the envelope pouch closed.

Sophia opened the pouch and turned it upside down into her palm. Out spilled an old pewter thimble with tiny bumps all raised around the fingertip.

"Oh, Tessie," were the only words Sophia could say.

"Your Memi wanted you to have it," Tessie said as she nodded.

"Tessie, I was so mean to you. How can you give me this or anything?" Sophia said softly while looking into the little candle's flame.

"Sophia, I want to explain something to you. Sometimes it's lonely and even a little sad for your Poppy and me without your Memi and Uncle Max. So together we reminisce and tell stories and sometimes we even laugh. He is a lifelong friend to me, Sophia. And that's what he will always be. Just like Thomas is for you." Tessie spoke softly as she placed her hand on Sophia's arm.

The lights of all the cottages in the circle began to flicker on. Sophia put her head back in the chair and took in a deep breath. She felt lighter and even a little happier, even while she still missed Memi.

"I am sorry, Auntie Tessie. I just miss Memi and I thought you and Poppy forgot her," Sophia said softly.

"Sophia, you are a kind girl with a big heart like your Mem. You can carry her with you always. Once in a letter Memi wrote to me after you were born, she shared that she loved your new name. Do you know what your name means, Sophia?" Tessie asked as she pulled her sweater closed around her.

"No, I don't. What does it mean?" Sophia whispered.

"You have a special name and one that is fittingly yours. Sophia means *wisdom*."

## Chapter Nine

Sophia woke up the next morning to the sound of voices outside her window. She pulled up her window shade and saw Tessie working in her garden. Poppy had just placed his fishing gear against the side of her fence and joined Tessie in her garden area. Poppy started to help her tie the tall tomatoes to the wooden stake assigned to each plant. Sophia watched and picked up the teapot and placed it on her lap. She opened the lid and gently reached in. One by one she pulled out the five little things; the old brass key, the sapphire sea glass, the mother-of-pearl button, the glass ladybug, and the pewter thimble. She carefully placed each one on her pillow in a row. She opened the memory book and wrote one line, *The little things will always matter most of all.* And then one by one she placed each little thing back into the teapot and put it back next to the apron on the side table.

Sophia walked out to the kitchen and saw a basket on the table. She peeked under the faded blue dish towel. Tessie's chocolate chip muffins. She pulled two mismatched plates and two glasses from the cupboard and set the table. First she sat on the bench seat but couldn't sit still. She hopped up and walked to the porch door. Sophia saw Poppy walking up the path toward the cottage. He had his fishing pole in one hand and a stringer of fish in the other. He plopped the fish in a bucket by the side fence. Poppy paused, tipped his fishing hat to his granddaughter, and then walked up the steps to the cottage.

Poppy nodded when he saw the table set for two. Without any words, he sat down and poured juice for both of them. Poppy cleared his throat and Sophia looked at him. He did not say anything, though. Not for a while at least.

Sophia placed a warm muffin on each of their plates. She looked quickly at Poppy, wondering if he was going to talk.

"I miss her. Your Memi meant everything to me. And I will never forget her."

Sophia could not speak. All of her words were locked in her throat. She pushed her chair back quickly, almost toppling it over, and went to stand next to Poppy's chair. He placed his arm around her waist. She leaned her curly-top head on his shoulder for a while.

"I miss her too, every day. It's OK that it's different, Poppy. We'll be OK, won't we?"

"Yes, Sophia, we will. We will."

After a few moments Sophia sat back down, and she and Poppy finished their breakfast in silence. But it was a kind of silence that was peaceful, not hollow. Suddenly the cottage circle exploded into a noisy celebration. The crunching sound of car tires on the shell-covered driveway, the honking of horns, and silly whooping hollers. Sophia and Poppy looked at each other and smiled. For a moment Sophia wished she had the rest of the week all to herself.

Just as Sophia was ready to dash out of the porch door to greet everyone, she quickly ran back to her little room. She took the teapot from the nightstand and plopped down on the edge of the bed. Sophia's heart was racing. She needed another minute of quiet before the others came crashing in. She lifted the little knob to open the teapot lid and hastily reached in. She swirled her hand around in the belly of the teapot, closed her eyes, and whispered Memi's name. Sophia's fingers then pinched up the pearl button like an arcade game claw. She quickly placed the button in her pocket. And for that day, and every day after, Sophia kept something of Memi's with her always to remember.

For Tommy—a lifelong friend and an amazing
artist. With vivid sight and sound and smell,
I remember the endless adventures of
a magical place we knew simply as *in back
of the fence*. Your courage and creativity are a
blessing and an inspiration always.

For my trusted "go-tos"—
long with me on this journey to print.
You all matter – and all believed. With my sincerest
gratitude…

And for my B's…we are all connected. Here and after.
Remember them always, wherever they may be.
We're never alone.

CPSIA information can be obtained at www.ICGtesting.com
Printed in the USA
LVOW12s1751051114

412174LV00007B/1028/P